A Walk through Heaven

JACQUES E. LAFRANCE

A Walk Through Heaven
Copyright © 2023 by Jacques E. LaFrance

Published in the United States of America
ISBN   Paperback: 979-8-89091-233-6
ISBN   eBook: 979-8-89091-234-3

All rights reserved. No part of this publication may be reproduced, stored in a retrieval system or transmitted in any way by any means, electronic, mechanical, photocopy, recording or otherwise without the prior permission of the author except as provided by USA copyright law.

The opinions expressed by the author are not necessarily those of ReadersMagnet, LLC.

ReadersMagnet, LLC
10620 Treena Street, Suite 230 | San Diego, California, 92131 USA
1.619. 354. 2643 | www.readersmagnet.com

Book design copyright © 2023 by ReadersMagnet, LLC. All rights reserved.

Cover design by Tifanny Curaza
Interior design by Don De Guzman

Illustrations by Laurie Brumbaugh

Preface

This is a work of fiction. I have never died and experienced the things in this story. However, some of the things in my life apart from the heaven experiences are true. So in that sense this is partly autobiographical although still overall a fictional account.

The heaven experiences are all based on actual eyewitness testimony recorded in *Heaven Is Beyond Imagination*. Even though the story as a whole, my journey in paradise, is fiction, everything it says about heaven is true based on eyewitness testimony. I have taken upon myself many of the things the eyewitnesses to heaven say about their experiences there as I reported in my previous nonfiction book *Heaven Is Beyond Imagination*. So that part of this story is true although it is not true of me. I have never personally experienced what is in this story but others have.

My hope is that in reading this story that is based on real experiences you will be able to see a picture of heaven to which you can relate. It is told from the point of view of a single individual, me, rather than a collection of separate individuals. Perhaps you can imagine a walk through heaven with me as I make this fictitious journey. If you have lost a loved one, I hope my narrative gives you joy and peace imagining your loved one experiencing the same things, perhaps even you walking with him or her.

I would still encourage you to read what I reported from the others in *Heaven Is Beyond Imagination*, as you will get a much more complete idea of the alternative views of things in heaven from different people's perspectives.

"I Want To Stroll Over Heaven With You"
by Alan Jackson

If I surveyed all the good things that come to me from above
If I could count all the blessings from the storehouse of love
I'd simply ask for a favor of Him beyond mortal kin
And I'm sure that He'd grant it again

I want to stroll over Heaven with you some glad day
When all our troubles and heartaches are vanished away
Then we'll enjoy the beauty where all things are new
I want to stroll over Heaven with you

So many places of beauty we long to see here below
But time and treasures have kept us from making plans as you know
But come the morning of the rapture together we'll stand anew
While I stroll over Heaven with you

I want to stroll over Heaven with you some glad day
When all our troubles and heartaches are vanished away
Then we'll enjoy the beauty where all things are new
I want to stroll over Heaven with you
I want to stroll over Heaven with you

I awoke early that Friday morning, got out of bed, walked to the window, and looked out on a lovely moonlit spring morning with the trees beginning to bud and wildflowers blooming in the grass, primarily the yellow dandelions and the beautiful but sparse purple henbit. As I looked across the yard, the purple henbit made it look like a purple carpet covering the yard, with occasional yellow buttons attached. There was an orange glow above the eastern horizon that told me dawn would soon be here. Although it was faint twilight I could see the lightly wooded landscape clearly. In fact, I had never seen the yard this clearly early in the morning before. It was as clear and bright as midday and I was amazed.

Three weeks before I had discovered a fuzzy spot in the central vision of my left eye causing distortions and obscurations in my detailed vision. I made an appointment with my optometrist, and she examined my eye saying I had a bubble on my retina that was causing the distortions.

"What is causing the bubble," I asked.

"Fluid, probably blood, has leaked out," she said.

"Then it is like a blood blister?"

"Yes."

"I guess it would require surgery to drain the fluid."

"The retina specialist I am sending you to will probably try external treatments to drain the fluid first. If the bubble breaks, it would cause a hole in your retina."

"I don't want a hole in my central vision. I would not be able to read with that eye."

"You have a hole in the retina of your right eye, but it is off to the side."

"I didn't know. I have never noticed it."

So I have an appointment with a retina specialist next week. Immediately after this news, I prayed, "Lord I ask you for healing of the retina in my left eye. When you walked the Earth you gave clear vision to a man blind from birth. You gave another clear vision although it took two tries. Another was told to wash his eyes in the pool, and he got clear vision. So I know you can heal my retina, and I know you want me to be in the health you designed for me. Having clear vision is one of the things you designed in our bodies, and I know that is what you want for me. You told many, 'Your faith has healed you.' So I believe you will heal my eye. I know you have heard my prayer, and are in the process of making it happen. I thank you for the healing."

While I was looking out at the yard in the morning light, I covered my right eye and did not see any distortion with my left eye. Wherever I looked, everything was perfectly clear. "Halleluiah!" I thought, "God has healed my retina!"

Then I realized I was not wearing my glasses, yet I was seeing everything clearly, no matter how far away it was. I have always been nearsighted and have never seen distant things clearly without my glasses. But now I was seeing as far as I wanted with perfectly clear vision without my glasses. Somehow God had restored my eyes to 20/15 or better without corrective lenses. I looked closely at my left hand and saw it just as clearly, so I had perfect near vision also. I praised God again for more healing than I had requested, both clear distant vision and clear near vision without any glasses. His healing of my eyes went far beyond what I would have imagined.

Then I noticed something else. I had had a place on my hand that would scab over, then the scab would come off (usually with my help!), and then scab over again. But lately it quit scabbing over and just became a small hard lump that was painful when bumped or pressed. I exclaimed, "Now it is gone. God has healed that also!"

"God, somehow during the night you have healed everything I knew that needed healing and some things I had not thought about. I praise you again."

As I looked at the bed I saw that I had not thrown the covers aside when I got up. It was like I had just slid through them without rearranging them. Weird! I have sometimes slid out from under the covers, but they are always somewhat rearranged afterwards. These were not.

But they were kind of humped up, so I looked much closer and saw a face. It was a mirror image of the face I had seen in the mirror many times. It was my face! That lump in the bed covers must be me but I am standing here by it. How can that be me when I am standing here looking at me?

I poked it and said, "Me, wake up! It's me." There was no response, but as I thought about it, that was probably good. If the me in the bed had responded while I was standing there looking at me, I would have faced a major philosophical dilemma as to which was the real Me and whether it was at all possible for me to exist simultaneously in two persons. If there were two "me's", which one was the one through which I was experiencing the sensations. If it were both, I could pinch the other me and feel it myself! I did not know how that could be possible. My vision and feelings and consciousness can only exist in one body at a time. How could my consciousness be aware of two different visual sensations at the same time from different perspectives? My real self would have to keep trading places back and forth to exist in two persons and it could never be simultaneous.

That leads me to only one conclusion; my spirit has separated from my body as in death. Am I really dead? How can I be dead when I feel more alive than I ever have before and all my physical conditions have been healed and perfected? The only way to find out if I am dead is to feel my pulse, but there is no pulse in the spirit body I am dwelling in now. The spirit body had nothing physical about it so I can feel no pulse in it. I can't actually touch my physical body in a way to detect a pulse, so I can't detect a pulse there either. The spirit body is now the one through which I am experiencing life, or whatever this is. I feel more alive that I ever have, so it is definitely not death. But some things are radically different (in a good way). So I do not know what has happened to me. I can't know whether I am dead or just separated from my body that is still alive somehow.

Suddenly there was someone in a shining white robe next to me.

I said, "Hello, where did you come from?"

"I am your guardian angel. I have come to take you to see the Master who wants to show you His kingdom."

"What is your name?"

"I am Jacob."

"That is interesting. Jacob is the Hebrew for Jacques."

"Yes, I know. We chose to name you Jacques so you can follow your namesake."

"But my parents gave me that name after my mother's niece suggested it."

"I know. I was the one that put it in your aunt Dorene's mind to suggest 'Jacques' to your mom. It was all part of God's plan, just as this visit is. "

"You said, you are going to show me His kingdom? Where is that? How do we get there?"

"I will be taking you there. And I can't say where it is that you can understand."

"Why can't I understand? I have studied many branches of science: astronomy, physics, geology."

"The science you studied here will do you no good where we are going. You are going to visit the Father's kingdom. God has asked you to go there in place of many others and for them, just as Jacob took his brother's place in the inheritance and blessing. You will see many things and come back to tell His people what He has prepared for them."

With that we suddenly were out of the house and traveling at a great speed somewhere. But there was no wind and we flew past stars and galaxies.

"Where are we going," I said as I became aware I had no control over what I was doing. Someone else was directing my travels.

"God's kingdom is not part of this universe. We are traveling outside of space and time to get to the Father's kingdom.

"Some people just instantly appear there, but God wants you to have this journey."

"Have I died and am going to heaven?"

"The Father has chosen you to have this visit so you can write about it and tell others so they will be prepared to come here."

"Have I died? If I have, how will I tell others?"

"You are visiting temporarily and will need to return to your earthly life. I will be with you to make sure you keep all your appointments and get you back to your earth life. The angel Maldorf will be your main guide to tell you what the Father wants you to know."

I saw a bright light in the distance. As we got closer I saw that the light seemed to emanate from the center of a large city. As we approached it, I saw a magnificent city with golden buildings and streets. There were trees and waterways, and magnificent houses among the waterways. There was a large wall around the city with many villages and parks outside. There were forests and hills, and I even saw mountains with something like pure white snow on them.

We slowed for a landing. As geese coming in to land on a pond, we came in and landed on a green grassy hill outside the wall.

The grass on this hill was the most beautiful shade of green I had ever seen. It was a vibrant pure green with no blemishes or discoloration. I saw no brown leaves anywhere I looked. The whole hillside looked like a perfectly manicured lawn. I don't think even the greens and fairways at the Masters Golf Tournament look any better. The blades of grass were about three inches long and were the same size for as far as I could see. I saw that I was barefoot and the blades of grass came up through my foot. I looked back and saw I was not leaving any footprints in the grass. The grass was undamaged by my walking on it. Then I became aware that the grass was transmitting energy to me up through my legs. The grass was alive in a way grass on Earth never is. I saw, too, that there were flowers throughout the field of grass. "It is so beautiful! I have never seen anything this beautiful on Earth."

Jacob said, "You are going to see more of the flowers as well as trees and many other aspects of God's Kingdom later. We have other things to explore first."

I also noticed I was wearing an attractive white robe. I don't know from where the robe came, as I don't have one like this in my home. From the time I first got up and looked out the window, I was unaware of my clothing or whether I was naked. The "me" in bed seemed to be clothed in my regular nightclothes. So I said to Jacob, "I see I am wearing a nice white robe. I don't have such a robe. Where did this one come from?"

He said, "Everyone who comes to heaven is given a white robe of righteousness. You will wear it for each encounter with the Father or the Son at the throne. You will be given other garments for other occasions, even some like you would normally wear on Earth, when you come here permanently. The white robe represents that you have been washed perfectly clean by the blood of the Lamb."

I was awed and didn't know what to say. It all left me speechless.

The walk up the hill was effortless, unlike climbing hills on Earth. There was no huffing and puffing. I was a runner in high school and college, but it feels like I could now do as much or more than my best days in track. The air was fresh and had a pleasant fragrance, perhaps like the taste of strawberries and cream. I became aware of wonderful music in the air. It seemed to be coming from a choir nearby. Then I saw what looked like a cloud but it was a band of angels drifting across the sky making the music singing hymns of praise. Some I knew and some I had never heard before. It was all incredible and mind-boggling. The grass, the flowers, the music, the air, and my new capabilities, were all better than I could have imagined. Perhaps that is why when people experience something really great, they say it is heavenly or like being in heaven. But no matter how good it is, no Earthly experience can compare with what I have already experienced here.

Then I saw that we were not alone. Suddenly another angel was walking with us.

Jacob said, "Jacques, this is Maldorf. He is going to be our guide to explain everything to you."

"Hi Maldorf. Thank you for what you will be sharing with me."

He said, "My pleasure, Jacques. We always do what the Father bids us do and He told me to be your guide on this visit to explain everything to you. I will tell you all I am permitted to tell, but there will be some things I will not be able to share."

"Why is that?"

"You are only visiting and there will be some things you are not permitted to see or know. That is the Father's command, and no one ever disobeys God here."

As we walked along beside the wall I noticed colorful stones: pink, green, blue, amber, and others. I remember John described the wall in Revelation as having multiple layers of exquisite gems. I don't know gems very well so I don't know if these are the same ones John saw. But these were huge, maybe twelve to eighteen inches in diameter and football shaped. On Earth they would probably be worth more than all the wealth of the world combined. Light from the city shown through the stones and cast multiple colors on the grass outside. Then I became aware that the wall was humming along with the angel choir. I mentioned this to my guides.

Maldorf said, "Everything in heaven is alive with the love and light of God. Everything in its own way gives forth praise to God."

This reminds me of Psalm 114:10, "All you have made will praise you, O Lord," and Luke 19:40, "'I tell you,' he replied, 'if they keep quiet, the stones will cry out.'" In heaven it is really true that all God has made is praising Him. It is a new and surprising thing to me to realize inanimate objects, such as a stone wall, can express praise.

We came to a gate in the wall. It was large, like everything I was seeing in heaven. It appeared to be a giant pearl or pearl-like material with gold decorations on it. There was an angel at the gate with a large book. He looked in the book as we approached.

"What is he doing," I asked.

Maldorf said, "He is looking in the Book of Life for your name."

"How does he know me?"

"God knows everything about you and has given the knowledge of who you are to the angel."

"Welcome, Jacques of the family LaFrance. Your life started September 25, 1938 and were born the second time November 13, 1957."

"But I was born June 25, 1939."

"God records the day you were conceived and received your full complement of DNA as the date you began life, not the date you emerged from your mother's womb. These are the only two dates important in your record, although the records in the God archives contain many other dates."

"What about the date I die or died?"

"That is only important for the records on Earth. From God's point of view, you will never die now that you have been born again in the spirit. You will just transition from God's proving ground on Earth to your heavenly home here where you will live for eternity."

I remembered that when I got up, I felt more alive when I was out of my body than I ever was when I was in it. It is really true that the real "me" is my eternal spirit and the temporary body is just a shell in which my spirit lives during my training days on Earth.

Then the angel at the gate touched the center of the pearl and it dissolved from the center out to create a great opening. I saw through the opening the most beautiful city I had ever seen with people joyfully playing, singing, and interacting with each other. There was a joy and peace and acceptance in that city that I had never seen on Earth. My whole being longed to enter and join in the wonderful experience they were all having. Then the angel asked, "Do you want to come in?"

Jacob then said, "You can't go in. If you ever go through the gate you can never return. But you are to return to Earth and follow the Father's bidding for you."

I told the angel, "I really want to enter, but this is not my time. Next time I come I will enter."

"So be it," said the angel; "We will hold your place for you." The pearl then flowed back together and closed the gate.

I turned to go back down the hill and there in front of me was a large crowd of people, including many I knew who had died earlier.

"Where did all these people come from?" I asked.

Jacob said, "They are your welcoming committee. God told them you were coming and to meet you here."

In the crowd I saw many people who had been a part of my life but had passed on. I saw my dear grandparents who had lived in Adrian, a small town south of Kansas City. I had spent many happy hours there as a child, watching the rain drops falling from their front porch making quarter-sized bubbles in the pools, tinkering in my grandfather's carpenter shop, making toy cars out of scrap strips of quarter-round, visiting the numerous half brothers and sisters of my granddad on their small farms, using an outhouse with an old Sears catalog for paper at my aunt's home, getting water from a pump well, and many others. The seeds of the Gospel were planted when I attended vacation Bible school at their Methodist church. I saw my first wife, Kennalee, who had been murdered when she was 56. She came up to me with a huge smile, embraced me with a tight warm hug.

"I am glad to see you," I said, "you look just like you did in the vision God gave me of you after you were gone. He showed me a love and joy in you and a peace and wholeness and freedom from all the emotional struggles you had. You looked more beautiful and peaceful and whole than I had ever seen in you before. Now, here you are looking the same."

"Yes, God has totally healed me and given me joy and peace I had never known. Coming here has been a wonderful gift."

"When I had that vision, you told me that God was pleased with me. Even though I didn't think I had been a good husband. I knew then that all was forgiven; God's slate was clean. That was very healing for me."

"God was pleased that you listened to the Holy Spirit and forgave Johnny. That is all that matters, that you follow the Holy Spirit. All the wrongs you have done are totally forgiven and you are not to dwell on them. God does not remember them. Instead always seek what God wants of you now. "

"When I had that vision, I could see that all was well with you, as I see it now in you. God has truly blessed you."

"Yes, I am, and you are going to be honored and blessed here, too, if you keep listening to the Holy Spirit and following God's leading. Don't worry about the sins you make, they are already forgiven, and God is ready to give you victory whenever you let Him. Enjoy this visit here and be sure to take back all God wants you to share with His people on Earth."

"Good-bye. I will look forward to seeing you again here someday."

Next I saw my brother Pat who was killed in Viet Nam. I never knew if he had accepted the Lord.

"Hi, Pat! I am so glad to see you here. What has it been like for you?"

"I am glad to see you, too, Buster (the name I was called as a kid). I know you are just here for a visit, but when you come back we can do many things together. How is Chris (Pat's widow) doing?"

"Your death was very hard on her. Charlie stayed in touch with her more than I did. I heard from her last year and I think she is alright now."

"I have been following her life from here and speaking to the Lord in her favor. So He has given her some good times and blessed her. We have access to Jesus and the Father any time we wish and I have sought Him on her behalf many times. She has not been as alone as she has thought."

"This appears to be an amazing place."

"There is more love here than you can imagine. God's love permeates everything and radiates from it. All here have a wonderful love relationship with Jesus, the Father, and everyone here. You can never experience this much love on Earth. It is the one thing that causes people never to want to leave."

"So why do some go back after they have experienced this wonderful place?"

"Some like you are required to go back. You have only been brought here temporarily because God has a mission for you back on

Earth. You are to tell people what God has prepared for those who love and follow Him. They need to get ready spiritually because Jesus is coming back very soon and they need to have the faith and endurance to resist Satan's final onslaught against God's people before then.

"Others choose to go back because someone there needs them."

"That is all amazing. How do you know so much?"

"You are going to see places of learning here. There is an infinite amount of God's knowledge and there is infinite time to learn. You will be learning all the time you are here, and being in the presence of Jesus and God's love all the time allows His knowledge to be given to you far better than can ever happen on Earth."

Jacob, "Come on Jacques. There are others we need to meet and other places to go."

"Ok, bye Pat. I will see you again."

"Bye Jacques. Be sure to trust and listen to the Holy Spirit. You have a mission to fulfill before you come back. I will be supporting you."

Some of my relatives, many of whom I had never met, were there to welcome me to heaven.

My college roommate Laurie was there, beaming with joy, cured of all the emotional hang-ups he had had. And my friend and cross-country teammate, John Evans, gave me a warm embrace of joy. He had accepted Jesus when I took him to Youthtime (Youth for Christ) at the Park Street Church in Boston my freshman year. He later became a minister and pastored in Pennsylvania the rest of his life. There were many others, all beaming with joy and happiness at meeting me. The joy and love in the air was astounding. I had never known such love and acceptance before.

My grandmother explained, "We were told you would be coming and to meet you here. We normally meet new arrivals the moment they set foot in paradise, but since you will be just a visitor, God wanted you to see this glimpse of heaven before meeting us. When you come back permanently we will all be waiting at the entrance portal, and there will be more besides us. Everyone who ever had a part in your growth as a Christian will be here to welcome you."

My guardian angel, Jacob, said, "We need to move on. We have much to see before you return to your earth life." So I said a very warm good-bye to all.

Someone said, "Remember the Lord always and what He has done for you."

Many shook my hand and embraced me, saying, "Love the Lord and pass His love on to His people. We will see you again later."

We went back down the green grassy hill to a park-like area in the countryside. There were flowers everywhere, some looked like flowers I knew but others were completely different. But even the flowers that were like some I had seen on Earth were different. They were brighter and more colorful. The colors were richer and deeper than any flowers on Earth. All the flowers were perfect; there were no deformed flowers.

Maldorf said, "You can pick a flower." So I picked one that looked like a sunflower. When I held it up to my face, I sensed that it was smiling at me. I had never heard of flowers having emotions and smiling before. Then I heard the flower humming a praise melody like everything else I encountered. It reminded me again of Psalm 145:10, "All you have made will praise you, O Lord;" The flower gave forth a wonderful aroma, different from any I knew but kind of like lavender or lilac.

Maldorf said, "Put the flower back down and it will be planted and continue growing."

So I set the flower back on the ground and it was immediately planted just like it had been before I picked it. He explained, "Nothing dies in heaven, not even flowers. That flower will keep blooming forever. Even if you put it in a vase or fasten it to the wall, it will keep growing and being beautiful."

As I looked around I saw many flowers all over the field of grass. They were all more colorful and beautiful than any
flowers on Earth and none had any blemishes. The colors were brighter and more vivid than on Earth. And there were colors unlike any on Earth, many more than we have on Earth. As I walked by, all the flowers turned as if to face me and look at me. The sight, sound, aroma, and feeling of those flowers were amazing!

Then we came to some trees. Most had leaves but some trees were more like evergreens. They reminded me of Western Red Cedar. Like the grass and the flowers, there were no dead limbs or leaves. All the leaves were green and beautifully shaped. There were no dead limbs or leaves on the ground. Maldorf said, "Again I tell you, nothing ever dies in heaven, not flowers, not trees, not leaves, not humans, not animals, not anything."

I saw a huge absolutely fascinating tree.

Maldorf said, "That is a Diadem tree. It has been growing since this garden was made. It is much older than Methuselah, the 4856-year-old bristle cone pine that is currently the oldest known living thing on Earth."

Each leaf was shaped like a crystal chandelier teardrop. As the leaves brushed against one another in the gentle breeze, it made a continual beautiful sound of crystal chimes. As the sound emanated from a leaf, there was a glow. Each leaf, each limb of the entire tree gave off a tremendous glow with all the colors that I had seen in Heaven, causing the tree to glow with sound and light, aflame with glory. The glory flame started in the root and went all the way up the tree and out through the branches to the chandelier-like leaves. The tree exploded in a beautiful lighted cloud of glory and an unbelievably beautiful sound. The Diadem tree was glorious. There were tens of thousands of people worshipping God under it. There were more such trees just as glorious.

One of the trees was like a walnut tree. It had pear-shaped copper-colored fruit on it. Maldorf said, "Take one and eat it."

I was uncertain about eating something I had never seen before, but I assumed Maldorf knew it would be all right. When I touched the fruit to my lips, it evaporated and melted into a delicious juice that was like honey, peach juice, and pear juice. It was sweet, but not sugary. It immediately ran down my throat like honey. It was the most delicious thing I had ever tasted. The juice from the fruit was all over my face, but in the atmosphere of heaven, it was gone instantaneously.

Maldorf told me, "Nothing ever gets soiled in heaven. Whatever stains you automatically evaporates and leaves you clean. Whatever goes down your throat totally disappears with nothing to eliminate from your body. No one sweats here no matter how hard one exercises. Bathrooms are not necessary and no houses in heaven have bathrooms."

"Wow!" I said, "That is certainly different. It would be nice never having to go to the bathroom. But where would I shave?"

"You will never need to shave in heaven or have a haircut or any other personal maintenance function," Maldorf said.

Then he showed me some other trees. They were growing beside a river and all had many fruits on them, some like a Bartlett pear, but larger.

I asked, "Is it okay to eat these fruits? Will I get sick?"

Maldorf explained, "On Earth everything needs nutrition to facilitate the production of new cells to replace worn out ones and to give the plant or animal energy for life. None of that is needed here. There are no cells and nothing dies and needs nutrition or replacement. The power of God supplies all the energy anything needs."

"Does that mean we do not have to eat?"

"That is correct."

"But doesn't the Bible suggest there is food in heaven?"

"There is food in heaven, delicious food, better food than the best on Earth. But it is a gift of love from God for your pleasure. It has nothing to do with being alive. In fact, your spirit body has no alimentary canal with digestive organs so it is impossible to digest the food you eat."

"I don't get it. How can I eat if the food has no place to go in me?"

"You are thinking like an Earthling. Here you can eat all you want or nothing at all if you wish. When you do eat, it is for pleasure, not nourishment. After you have had the pleasure of the food, it just vaporizes. You never have anything left over to eliminate."

"So I can fast forever and never die, but I can also gorge myself with food and never have to use a restroom or get sick. Is that what you are telling me?"

"Yes, your life here is eternal. Nothing can ever cause it to cease and you never have any discomfort. Fasting or gorging will not harm you, so just eat what you enjoy of whatever you want. As to using a restroom, that is never needed here. In fact, as I said before, none of the homes or buildings have bathrooms; they are not needed."

"How do I take a bath or clean up if there is no bathroom?"

"In heaven you never get dirty and need to clean up. If you want to enjoy water, you go to one of the rivers, lakes, or sea. You will see more about those later on our trip, and you will get to enjoy what the waters in heaven are like."

I picked one of the Bartlett pear types of fruit and tested it. It was delicious, more so than any pear I had ever eaten. It had a consistency and flavor similar to the finest frozen cream. Another fruit was in clusters that were also pear-shaped, but smaller than the previous one. A third fruit was shaped like a banana. I picked one of the banana-like fruits and Maldorf said, "That is called a breadfruit. Taste it and tell me what you think."

I did and said, "It tastes like a dainty finger-roll."

The branches all had many fruits and all were within reach of people coming to them. Children were gathering fruits to take back to their families, (Yes, there are children in heaven. I'll tell you more later.) Others were picking fruits and eating them like I just did. And none needed to wash their hands or face. Then I observed a miracle I had not expected: another fruit grew in the place of the one that I had picked.

Maldorf said, "After you have enjoyed the taste and smell of the food, it just evaporates. So stomach and intestines are not needed.

"God constantly provides all the food anyone could want at no cost, a free gift of His love. In fact, no one has to eat in heaven, but God provides delicious food just for our pleasure."

Then I looked at my body and saw that it was translucent. I could see the grass beneath me. I could see through my body and see that I had no internal organs, no stomach, no intestines, no liver, no heart, no blood, no bones, etc.

I panicked and exclaimed, "I am sick! Something happened. How can I survive?" I temporarily forgot about Maldorf's statement about not having any digestive organs.

Maldorf calmed me saying, "Calm down. Nothing is wrong with you. Your body is not biological like it is on Earth. Biological bodies made with molecules decay and don't survive. Your heavenly body is not made with molecules that break down and will never decay. Hence there is no need for digestion and all the organs that are necessary to keep the body alive. You are fully alive here without any problems of disease or decay. You are perfect, the way God intended you to be."

I recovered from the shock that all my internal organs, including my heart, were gone and realized that, in fact, I am more alive and healthier than I have ever been. My spirit body is much better than my physical body. I reflected on the fact I observed at the beginning that my vision is better than it has ever been. Even without my hearing aids, I am hearing many times better than I did with them, and I am hearing tones much higher and lower than I could before. All my senses are much sharper than they were before.

At that time a dog, a mix of yellow lab and golden retriever, came bounding up to me and licked my face. I recognized it immediately as my dog Sunny, who was always eager to see me and to go wherever I went.

"Hi Sunny!" I exclaimed.

"I am glad to see you again my master."

"You can talk and speak in ways I can understand?"

Maldorf explained, "Yes, since all communication is by thought and not speech, animals can communicate as well as humans. Vocalizations are used for singing praises but not for communication; voices are not needed for talking. You will see more examples of animals and people communicating."

Sunny continued, "I know you are just visiting, but I had to see you anyway. I have been playing a lot with Shadow, and he will see you when you come back."

I told my angel friends, "We rescued Shadow, a black lab, from Mohawk Park when he was an emaciated four-month old pup that had been living off of dried earthworms and acorns. Later we rescued Sunny as a slightly older pup from Mohawk Park. Sunny had taken to Shadow as his older brother and looked up to him, played with him, and enjoyed him. After Shadow died of a tick-born disease, Sunny had obviously missed him, and for a long time checked out other black labs he saw in case they were Shadow. One time as he got older, he saw a black lab across the street and ran to it, greeting it like a long lost brother. The other dog didn't seem to know what to do with this attention and largely ignored Sunny. However, Sunny seemed to think in his old age that this was, in fact, Shadow back and followed him down the street to the corner and a block or two around the corner until the other dog went into a wooded area. I had been following and after the other dog left, Sunny came back to me and I petted him, understanding that he was still feeling the loss of Shadow.

"Not long after that Sunny developed cancer behind his right eye, for which there was nothing we could do. His condition kept getting worse with him losing sight in his right eye and having to rub it a lot. Finally, his struggle had become so difficult we had him put to sleep. As he lay there on the vet's table I held him and told him several times he would see Shadow again very soon. That was a very sad time for my ex-wife and me.

"Now it is a joy to see that indeed Sunny has met Shadow and their previous friendship is flourishing. It brings tears to my eyes to think of it."

So I asked Maldorf, "Seeing that Sunny is here and hearing the Shadow is too, are all pets here?"

He said, "Every pet that has meant something to someone is here and ready to renew the relationship. And since all communication is mind to mind, spirit to spirit, everyone will be able to have conversations with their pets. In addition to the pets here, there are deer, foxes, lions, bears, various birds, turtles, fish, and even some insects. You might even see a snake or a dinosaur, but remember nothing here can hurt you. All the animals love you just as you do them here."

"Lions and bears! I would be afraid to meet up with one of them."

"You need have no fears. First of all, there is nothing fearful at all here, and nothing can hurt you. Remember the Scripture says, 'The wolf and the lamb will feed together, and the lion will eat straw like the ox.' (Ps 65:25) There are no hurts and nothing dies here. So no animals kill or injure other animals or people, nor do they want to.

"Since we don't have to eat here, and neither do animals, it doesn't matter what anyone eats. Eating is just for pleasure not nourishment. If we do eat, it is things God has made that do not require an animal to die. But you will find they are more delicious than anything on Earth involving animals.

"Come, I want to show you some other animals and pets."

We journeyed into a meadow in which there were horses.

Three horses came trotting over to see us: a white horse like Roy Rogers' Silver, a tan-colored horse, and a palomino.

I reached over and stroked the white horse. It said, "Thank you, that felt good."

I said, "These horses are beautiful and majestic. They look bigger and stronger and more beautiful than horses I have seen."

Over in another part of the meadow there was a young girl riding a horse. I could tell they were both very happy and enjoying each other. They were communicating, but I couldn't hear what they were saying.

In another part of the meadow I saw a pair of foxes romping and playing and four deer grazing.

I said to Maldorf, "You said we don't have to eat in heaven and neither do animals, so why are these deer grazing?"

He replied, "God loves all of His creation and just as you will enjoy eating delicious food here, so God lets the animals enjoy what they enjoy. These deer like to graze and so God has provided them with all the grazing they want to do. Just like the things you eat, after they have enjoyed the grass, it just vaporizes."

Then the most incredible sight to me was seeing three children playing with a male lion, climbing on it, riding it, and petting it. The lion was enjoying this as much as the children.

I said, "These children really seem to be enjoying this, just like the girl was enjoying the horse. Are all children like this here? What is life like here for children who died much too young on Earth?"

Maldorf said," Jesus said, 'Let the children come to me.' Jesus and the Father love children. You will be surprised at the wonderful life they have here. Come I will show you."

We then went to a park where we saw many groups of people eating, laughing, playing, singing, and really enjoying each other and their lives here. Some were talking, laughing, and singing; others were running around playing games, some were just enjoying the sights and sounds of heaven. Frequently I would hear someone call out, "Hi, Jacques. We are glad to see you here."

I replied, "Hi to you, too. I am glad to see how much you are enjoying life here."

"How do they know who I am?" I asked Maldorf. "I don't recognize any of them."

He replied, "Everyone here knows everyone else. We are one big family, the family of God. God enables everyone to know everyone else so we can all be together as one family."

"I have never seen such love for one another as I am seeing here. Just think how life on Earth would be so much better if people on Earth were this way also. I wonder if that is what it will be like on Earth when Jesus sets up His kingdom there for a thousand years or will it only happen in heaven where all sin is banished?"

Then I saw a group of children playing a game. They got in a circle with one child hovering over them in the center of the circle. (Heaven does not have gravity like that on Earth. There is gravity-like behavior, but different.) One child would push the hovering one and he or she would glide across the circle where another would push him or her back. There was lots of giggling and laughter. I wanted to join in their game!

Then I saw kids climb up a tree ten, twenty, or fifty feet up and jump out. That child would gently float to the ground like a cotton ball.

Maldorf told me, "Nothing in heaven can hurt you, nor can you be hurt by what you do. The children are perfectly safe."

"You keep reminding me that heaven is safe. I guess it is hard for us Earthlings to accept a concept so different from our earthly experience."

In another place the children were having contests. When they ran, they were faster than horses on Earth, and when they jumped they could go a hundred feet into the air and come down with a soft landing. These kids would all be Olympic champions on Earth.

I saw children who were old enough to walk and run and play, playing just like children do on Earth. It was like God intended for the children to play and have a good time and just be *children*. They were completely content just being children. They were experiencing a perfect childhood, which many adults here have missed.

I saw some play with animals and ride horses, with which they could communicate in thought, like the girl in the meadow on her horse I saw earlier.

"Oh, look! There are some kids sliding down a rainbow! How can they do that when a rainbow is just a refraction of light and not a tangible thing?"

Maldorf explained, "Some things were created for Earth to be images of the realm of heaven. Some things of heaven cannot be real in a physical world because they cannot be synthesized with atoms and molecules or the laws of physics. God has done a marvelous job creating the physical world of Earth to mirror many of the truths and beauties of heaven, but there is much more to heaven that cannot be experienced on Earth.

"God provided the mechanism for the rainbow, refraction of light through raindrops, to give Noah's people a sign that He would never again destroy the world with a flood. The mechanism for the rainbow is part of the physics of the physical world and as such is with you all the time on Earth, a symbol of God's love for His people."

I noted, "When I see all these people and their love and joy and companionship with everyone, I am overwhelmed with the fact that there is never any illness, pain, sadness, loneliness, or rejection in heaven, only unconditional love, acceptance, and joy."

Everyone loves the children and the children love everyone also. Love permeates heaven. It makes me want to go there and enjoy the contentedness and joy of a heavenly childhood.

Maldorf told me, "The children also attend school. They are taught the Bible and to read and write. They are taught arithmetic, philosophy, religion, and many other interesting subjects. They learn things geniuses on Earth could not possibly know or understand. Their intelligence in heaven is far above the highest level of intelligence on Earth."

We came to a building at the side of the park with soft blue and pink light shining across it in alternating waves and a play area.

Maldorf said, "This is heaven's nursery. This is where all miscarried and aborted babies come. Many angels and residents assist with taking care of these precious infants. The Father himself comes to love and raise these children. Even some animals are there attending to them. Some of the aborted ones wonder why their mothers didn't want them. They forgive their mothers and hope they forgive themselves. They look forward to seeing their parents some day. Do you want to go in and see them?"

"I would love to," I replied.

I said, "This little child is so small it fits in the palm of my hand, It is about the size of a lime but it has all the features of a child. Look, its little fingers and toes move!"

"Yes, it is twelve Earth weeks old. Its heart had been beating for nearly seven weeks. It died in its mother's womb two days ago. She didn't feel anything yet but her hormones have started changing so she will suffer emotionally from the loss of her child."

"I am sorry for the mom. Does the baby have a name?"

"No they didn't know their baby was a girl so they hadn't picked a name. Whatever name the parents give a child is the name the child will have for eternity in heaven. It is important to give your child a name. In cases like this, the parents can give it both a girl's and a boy's name and in heaven the correct one will be associated with that baby."

"Awesome! The baby is so cute and so little childlike. How can anyone not love the little guy, gal in this case? I never realized what an awesome responsibility the parents have in giving the child a name."

Maldorf went on, "The light of God is in each one of them and longs to be back with God. Here they are raised to spiritual maturity to become what God intended for them to be. Angels give excellent care for each baby. The angels sing to them and rock them, and the breath of God sustains them. They are raised in God's perfect love and are filled with joy.

"They mature much faster here than on Earth, but it is difficult to explain the passing of time to maturity in heaven since there is no time in heaven, it is always 'now.' And we can simultaneously experience events out of a time sequence."

"That is hard to imagine, I am so used to the passing of time on Earth."

Maldorf explained, "You live in a four-dimensional world with time as one dimension. Here time is multidimensional. Many things here are very different from Earth. There is no comparison in some cases like this.

"As they mature, they are very much like children on Earth."

I saw children of all ages in heaven. Some of them were the result of their mothers getting an abortion, others died of sickness, accident, or murder. All of them were at Jesus' feet and were peaceful, healthy, and happy, not a single sad face.

Many of the children I saw looked like newborns. In heaven, even the newborn babies have the power of speech and are completely responsive. They would know and understand what someone was saying to them and could reply. For me, this capability of children in heaven was amazing.

Then I saw Jesus with a group of children. He was hugging them and loving on them and they were all excited and loving him, too. I saw a little boy about one foot tall run up and jump into Jesus' arms. I couldn't hear what they were saying, but I could see love and joy in each of their eyes.

Maldorf told me, "Children here have capabilities children on Earth do not have. They can run and jump like this little boy and they can verbally communicate as well as an older person. Many are gifted artists or musicians."

I wanted to stay and enjoy seeing the children and all their fun, but Jacob said, "Come now, you need to see the River of life."

We walked over to the fruit trees again and Maldorf told me, "This is the River of Life. The fruit trees grow along the banks of this river and other places, too."

"This is the famous River of Life?" I asked, "It looks just like any river. What makes it special?"

Maldorf explained, "First it originates from under the throne of God and is an outgrowth of the creativeness of God that gives life to everything that lives. From there it winds its way through the city and out the east gate. It goes throughout heaven and gives heavenly life to all that encounter it."

"How does it do that?"

"I'll show you. Walk out into the river."

"But I don't have a swimming suit, just this lovely robe."

"Just wade out in your robe."

"I don't want to mess it up."

"You won't. Just go."

So I started out and got in up to my knees. The water had a different feel from any water I knew. It was like it was caressing me somehow. I can't really explain how it felt. It was so different from anything I had ever experienced. I waded out up to my waist and found the water to be both warm and cool in some way I can't explain. The pleasant feeling on my skin just kept getting better, kind of like getting a soft massage.

"Keep going," Maldorf said.

So by now I was up to my neck and I could tell there was more to this water, but couldn't tell what it was.

"Keep going," he said.

"But the water is already up to my neck, I'll drown!"

"You won't. Remember, nothing dies in heaven. Even beyond that, nothing in heaven can harm you in any way."

So I went in over my head and discovered I could breathe just as well under water as above it. I was beginning to enjoy this encounter and began examining the beautiful multi-colored rocks on the bottom of the river. I enjoyed being in the water and the river for a while and then waded back out.

"Where do I get a towel?" I asked.

"You don't need one," was the reply.

Sure enough, I found I was not wet. My robe was the same as before, and my hair was undisturbed.

"That is amazing!" I said. "That must not be water as in H_2O like we have on Earth, but a water-like substance that only exists here. Also it has done something to me, more than just a soothing massage."

"That is right," Maldorf said, "It is not earth water but heaven water, and it has washed away the last of your earth life to prepare you for life here. Everyone experiences this when they first come here. You will experience it again when you come permanently. At that time it will wash away all negative earth memories so nothing will spoil your full enjoyment of heaven. It hasn't done that completely for you now because you have to go back for a while."

Then I saw other people enjoying being in and beneath the water. Children were building rock castles on the bottom of the river.

"Are there other rivers like this in heaven?" I asked.

Maldorf replied, "There are more rivers and they are not all the same. There are also lakes and a sea, the Sea of God's Glory. Some people arrive here by way of the sea on boat-like conveyances and are greeted by their welcoming committees on the shore."

"Will I be able to see that?"

"That is our next stop," Jacob said to me.

Then we were suddenly walking out of a wooded area onto a beach with water, or whatever it was, stretching as far as I could see. There were multi-colored flowers blooming all the way to the water's edge. People were enjoying being in and under the water as they were in the River of Life.

"Can I try the water again?" I asked.

Maldorf and Jacob said in unison, "Yes, go ahead."

So I waded out into the lake and went in over my head. It was a delightful feeling and I was floating gently somewhere between the bottom and the surface. I watched two children gathering many multi-colored pebbles from the sea floor and an older man put the finishing touches on a castle made of rocks on the bottom of the sea.

I came up and went back to the shore. I felt very refreshed and Maldorf told me, "This water fills you to overflowing with a shower from the Celestial Life itself. "

"I don't know what that means, but I do feel very good and refreshed in some new way," I said.

As I stood there I noticed that the beach was many hundred feet wide and extended on either side far beyond what I could see. The beach caught and radiated the light, making it glitter and glimmer like diamond dust and other precious stones. The waves came and went in ceaseless motion, caught up this sparkling sand, and took it to their crests. The sea was spread out before me in a radiance that was beyond description. The waters of the sea had a blue tint, and there was no limit to its depth or bounds.

I saw boats in every direction, whose beauty far surpassed anything on Earth. They were like great, open pleasure barges and were filled with people looking eagerly toward the shore. Many were eagerly standing erect and gazing expectantly at the faces of those on the shore that were waiting for them.

The people on the shore stood as far as my eyes could see. The great throng was dressed in spotless gowns like mine. Many of them had golden harps and various instruments of music. When a boat touched the shore, the glad voices and tender embraces of their loved ones welcomed its passengers. Then the harps would be held up, and the vast multitude would break forth in a triumphant song of victory over death and the grave. I asked Maldorf, "Do people always stand here like this?"

He said, "It isn't always the same people, but there is always a crowd of people here who are expecting friends from the other life. They assemble to share in their joy. Some of the heavenly characters are always here, but not always the same ones. He said that their friends, and many others who are constantly joining the multitude, quietly lead away most of those who arrive."

I told my angels friends, "The water here, if that is the right word for it, is wonderful. It has done things for me that water on

Earth can't do. I guess the only reason to call it "water" is that is the most Earth-like thing that corresponds to it."

"You are right. It is very different from the water you know on Earth. Besides being spiritually cleansing and refreshing, if you drink some it will not be like tasteless Earth water, it will have a sweet flavor to it, not a sticky sweetness but a delightful smooth flavor. Also, there are two water-like liquids under the throne that are different, enough so that they do not mix. That is all I can tell you now."

"What other instances of water are there?"

"I will show you a falls and some fountains."

With that we were off to one of the other rivers. We came to a garden with a stream running through it. The stream came over a cascading waterfall.

Maldorf said, "Besides being dazzling, there is life in the water. Each drop has its own intelligence and purpose."

"How can an inanimate molecule have intelligence?"

"In heaven things are not as they are on Earth. Earth is like an architect's model. It looks like the real thing and in some ways functions like it, but it is just a model, very different from the real thing. So here, too, intelligence is an aspect of the spirit. You are a spirit, unencumbered by the physical body, so you can experience some of the spiritual reality here. Intelligence here goes way beyond what it is on Earth."

I heard a gentle quiet melody. I asked Maldorf, "Where is that melody coming from?"

"Each drop of the water as it flows over the falls sings a note of praise. All those notes together make up the melody you are hearing."

"That is amazing. I never imagined water making a melody, noise perhaps, but not a melody."

"Remember, here the scripture is fulfilled that says, 'All of creation sings praise to God.'"

"Do all the waters make melodies?"

"Everything does. I will show you one of the fountains and you can hear the music it makes."

There were many fountains, all very beautiful and significant. Maldorf led me to one that had a statue of Jesus with a cup pouring out a cup of glory. The water turned into ice but it was not cold and it changed colors. The music of all the drops together was a symphony that matched the changing colors.

I told him, "This just makes me want to hear more of the music in heaven. What I heard from the choir as I went up the green grassy hill, felt the wall, and heard the water, just inspires me to want to hear more."

I paid more attention to the music I was hearing. It seems like beautiful music is always in the air. Wherever I have gone from the first grassy hill to the city and then the park, I have been hearing beautiful praise music, both choral and instrumental. Other than the drifting angel choir I could not tell from where it was coming. It didn't originate from anywhere; it just emerged from everything and every place. But it was always there and always a great blessing.

I told Jacob and Maldorf, "Heaven is saturated with beautiful music. It brings joy and peace to my soul. I could listen to this music all the time."

Maldorf said, "It is the result of joy and expresses the happiness and joy of heaven."

I heard choirs and ensembles, whose splendor and beauty cannot be compared with anything on Earth. It is a fantastic symphony. Stringed instruments and trumpets accompany the music. All the voices, pitches, and tones were perfect.

I heard unbelievable anthems coming in waves of praise across the landscape. I heard many voices, melodious, harmonious, and blending in chorus. The singing included the word "Jesus". There were more than four parts in the harmony, and notes I never heard before. I heard multiple parts in other languages, with richness and perfect blending of the words. The amazing thing was that I could understand the words whatever the language!

Maldorf mentioned, "In the spirit in heaven you can understand all languages because they are thought to thought rather than voice to ear. There is also a heavenly language apart from all Earth languages. You will be able to understand them all."

The music had great diversity, and the intriguing melodies and their magnetic refrains played over and over in my spirit. Musical praise, comprised of melodies and tones I had never experienced before, was everywhere. The words of the songs were clear and meaningful. They spoke of honor, covenant, majesty, goodness, mercy, and truth. The music rang out with words such as "Hallelujah," "Praise," "Glory to God," and "Praise to the King," in the midst of all the music. I was awestruck and caught up in the heavenly mood. I experienced the deepest joy of my life. Even though I wasn't a participant in the worship, my heart rang out with joy and exuberance.

Thousands of songs were sung simultaneously, and they surpassed any I had ever heard. But in spite of all this different music being sung simultaneously, there was no chaos. I could hear each one and clearly discern the lyrics and melody.

I marveled at the glorious music and knew that if I sang too, it would be in perfect pitch and harmonious with the thousands of other voices and instruments. Even though on Earth I didn't have a great singing voice, there I could have sung in ways I never could on Earth. And the music was so powerful my spirit wanted to join in much of the time. Were it not for Jacob's schedule and my needing to pay attention to what Maldorf was showing me I might have stayed there and listened and sung myself!

But Jacob drew my attention back to what was happening at the park. "We must keep moving, Jacques, to stay on schedule and see everything God wants you to see.

They took me to the top of a high hill beyond the park.

Jacob said, "Look around, Jacques. What do you see?"

"I see the meadow where we saw the horses. From here I can see the full extent of the meadow. It is beautiful! The grass is so green and smooth. There are no bare or ugly places, no weeds, just beautiful grass. It is more than the grass I know; it is radiating God's glory in a way beyond what grass on Earth can do. Also, in the gentle breeze I feel, there are melodies coming from the grass and the flowers. There are flowers all over the meadow, like the ones I saw, but others besides. I have never seen such beautiful colorful flowers as these that are dotted throughout the meadow."

Then Jacob pointed my attention higher.

"I see many hills covered with wonderful forests. They look cool and inviting. They remind me of the spectacular Appalachian Mountains, but are much more spectacular. When I come back I want to take walks through those forests. From here I can't see individual trees very well, but they look like they would be as splendid as the ones you have shown me. I can imagine a walk through them would be cool and invigorating as well as being an amazing sight."

Maldorf said, "Yes, Jacques, heaven has wonderful meadows, forests, hills, valleys, and mountains, all comparable to similar features on Earth, but much grander. In addition, when you walk through them you will be exhilarated with praise and joy. God has not spared anything to make your life here superb."

I said, "You said, 'mountains'. I saw some mountains when I came into heaven. What are they like?"

"Yes there are mountains, some like the Sierras, some like the Rockies, some like the Alps."

"Can I see any of them?"

Jacob, said, "Yes, just hold onto my hand."

I took his right hand with my left and we started rising in the air.

I said, "Wait a minute, how can we just rise up in the air at will like this? Doesn't gravity hold us to the ground? What if we fall and get injured?"

Maldorf explained, "First of all, in heaven nothing can ever hurt you. You won't fall, but you might come down. Even so, you will land softly and never get hurt.

"Secondly, gravity here is not the same as on Earth. There is a gravity-like force that allows you to walk on the ground, although sometimes you will not actually walk but rather just glide along the ground. Even so, it doesn't bind you to the ground, and you can rise up in the air or travel through the air, whenever you wish. Remember the children playing where one child hovers above others in a circle and they joyfully push the suspended one back and forth across the circle of friends with much laughter and happiness? Heaven's gravity did not hold that child down on the ground. But when they jumped out of trees, the heaven gravity allowed them to come back down to the ground gently."

I said, "Yes, I remember all that. Heaven is indeed an amazing place, somewhat like Earth but different and superior in many wonderful ways.

"Now I see tall beautiful mountains, better than the Grand Tetons or the Alps. Many have snow on them. Are they cold enough the snow doesn't melt?"

Maldorf, "The 'snow' is not frozen water like it is on Earth. The water here is different. It is not H_2O as you learned at the River of Life. So it doesn't freeze or melt. The snow on those mountains is not frozen ice crystals and what it is never melts. Also the temperature there is comfortable, just like here."

"Can I ski there?"

"Yes, skiing is possible. It is one of the many activities enjoyed on Earth that you can do in heaven. But here you never have accidents and get hurt."

"Can I see?"

Jacob said, "No, there is no time for that. You can explore the mountains, skiing, and the forests when you come back permanently."

Maldorf, "Speaking of water and freezing, on Earth matter is either solid, liquid, gas, or plasma, but here there are other forms of matter as well. I can't show you because you have to go back to Earth, and you have not been cleansed of all your earthiness yet. The next time you bathe in the River of Life, all your earthiness will be washed away and then you will be able to know and understand many things about heaven that are not understandable to you now."

"I just noticed the sky over the mountains. It has the colors of a brilliant sunset but with other colors added. I thought there is no sun here, so how is there a sunset?'

Maldorf, "You are right, there is no sun. All light comes from within everything and is the light of the glory of God. The colors in the sky have been created by God just to make your stay here even better. Keep watching and you will see colored patterns that look like the auroras on Earth. And those clouds in the sky are actually groups of angels and people singing praises to God as they float by."

Jacob said, "It is time to move on. You need to see the mansions God has prepared for His people."

Suddenly there was a conveyance much like a bus, but it just hovered in the air rather than rolling on wheels. Jacob said, "Get in, it will take us to the next location."

Maldorf explained, "Conveyances like this have been made by someone who has the gift and desire to create them for the pleasure of residents. You can visit with others as you travel to your destination. Everyone exercises the gifts they had on Earth to be a blessing to others here."

Quickly and miraculously the conveyance took us back through the woods into the city and we were walking along one of its beautiful golden streets.

I said, "It looks like we are in the city, but we didn't go through the gate. Are we in trouble and I won't be able to go back?"

Maldorf explained, "It is true we didn't go through the gate, but God wants Jacob and me to show you some things in the city, so He permitted us to transport you here without going through the gate. We can show you around and then when we are finished, you will be going back to your Earth life."

I noticed that it looked like I was standing in water, but I felt no water on my feet. It was just that the street was as clear as water although golden also. I have heard the streets of heaven are paved with gold, but standing here on the street I can see it looks like gold but has clarity like water also. Whatever it is, it is neither gold nor water but something superior to both. Also I became aware of a hum in my feet as the street itself was echoing the praise of the angel choir above. The experience of this street of heaven is beyond anything at home with which I can compare it. It was a joy to experience this street.

I saw groups of flowers and beautiful trees all along this boulevard. The houses were all spectacular. Most had columns and verandas and wrap-around porches and were beautifully landscaped.

Maldorf explained, "Every house is made specifically for the one who will live there. It has the architecture and space that will most please the occupant. It will have whatever that person needs to continue the gifts he or she exercised on Earth: writing, singing, composing, teaching, preaching, researching, cooking, etc. Everyone will continue using the gifts God gave him or her on Earth in ministering to the body here. It will all be done as gifts and praise to the glory of God and love for everyone that is blessed. Everything here is given. There is no money or paying for anything. Everything we do is a gift of love to others. Everything you see here God has given freely to you and to all of us because His love is far greater than you can imagine. You can't earn it; you can't pay for it; you can't owe Him for it. It is that way with everything you do in heaven. However you use the gifts you have, what you do will be a free gift of love, just as all God has given to you is a gift of love."

"I will show you two houses," he said.

We walked further along that street and came to a two-story house with a small workshop attached to it at the back. It had a wraparound porch like many others I had seen. It resembled the old Bates mansion my grandparents had had in Adrian, Missouri. Then I saw Granddad and Grandmother sitting on the porch swing gently swinging and talking.

They saw me and shouted out, "Hi Buster (the name they had used for me), come up here and let us see you. You look very good, just like the little boy that came to visit and played at our house in Adrian."

"You both look better than I remember. You look like you are in your thirties."

"Yes, son, when each person steps into this hallowed land, all infirmities are healed, all age related effects are removed, and you are made to be in your prime of life. The change then lasts forever."

Granddad said, "Let me show you the workshop God has given me."

We went to the workshop that was attached to the house. He opened the door and there was the best collection of carpentry tools I had ever seen. Some were the finest hand tools like he had used and some power tools. There were also stacks of the most beautiful wood I had ever seen, better than the best mahogany on Earth. I am sure he had been making some absolutely beautiful furniture for other residents. I knew the work he had done on Earth, but what he could do here must be much better.

"Where do you get the electricity for the power tools?" I asked.

Granddad replied, "There is no electricity here. Everything is run by the power and light of God. This equipment is far better than anything I ever had in my life as a carpenter."

"I bet Grandmother's kitchen or sewing room is as good as this for her work. I am guessing that she can cook and sew better than anything she had done in her life on Earth, and that was pretty good."

Granddad said, "Yes Buster, we should have you here for one of her meals when you return. I know you are just visiting now and can't stay. But we will be looking for you later."

Jacob said, "We have to go."

So I said, "Good-bye Grandmother and Granddad. I am very glad to see you and I will look for you when I come back permanently."

"Bye Son. Stay true to the Lord and honor Him with all you do."

And off we went, turning onto a side street. Maldorf pointed out a house on the left side of the street. It was very different but very exquisite and beautiful. It appeared to be made of pearl.

Maldorf told me, "That house was carved out of a single large pearl. All of the fittings inside were also carved out of the pearl. This house was made for a missionary named 'Pearl.' She served the Lord her whole life and was destitute; giving everything she had to the poor she served. She had died of starvation. This was her reward for a pure heart."

"Can I look?"

"Yes, you may go up to the house and look in the window. If Pearl is there you can ask her if you can see the inside."

So I walked up to the house on the marble walkway lined with beautiful rose bushes and trees like redbuds in bloom. I looked in the large window on the porch and saw the magnificent chandelier hanging from the center of the ceiling. It was clearly part of the house and not an attachment. The furniture around the edge was also made of pearl and attached to the walls. There was some furniture in the room that was also pearl and had been carved in their locations. Besides the awesomeness of the carved furniture, the house was gorgeous, a fabulous place to live.

I wondered if she would like some very fine cabinets made by my Granddad.

These were the only mansions I was allowed to visit, but I saw many others that were more elaborate than the White House.

Maldorf continued what he had explained before, "In addition to making each person's mansion serve him or her in the best way, it is what makes him or her most comfortable, whether it is a large house, a cottage, or even a condominium. Those from other cultures usually prefer the kind of house they were used to. Whatever style it is, every home is optimum and beautiful for that person."

I saw city homes, rural homes, mountain homes with spectacular views, seaside homes, and many more. We didn't get to any area where we could see grass huts, if there are any, or other homes from different cultures on Earth.

Jacob said, "Now we are going to see some of the special buildings in this city."

Jacob started walking and I with him. We walked a short way and he pointed out the many buildings all also made of some gold-like substance that glowed with internal light. I saw no shadows because all the light comes from God and is internal to everything. Everything gives off the light of God internally. God's light is what illuminates heaven so there is no sun or moon or night. His light permeates everything and comes out of everything.

Maldorf pointed out the large archives building. He said, "Here angels keep all of God's meticulous records on every individual that has ever lived, recording everything they ever said or did or thought of saying or doing, even the things they didn't do."

I wondered, "How could He maintain such extensive records? It is mind-boggling!

"Could I see what it is like?"

"Let us go inside," he said.

It was a large hall with many levels of shelves extending as far as I could see. The books were stacked and there were so many I didn't see how one could find anything. There were many tall angels writing in the books with long quills about four feet long. Maldorf showed me the books with my name on them.

"Can I see what is written about me?"

"No, you are not permitted to see at this time. Some future events are already recorded and you are not allowed to know the future. But I will show you a few things."

I saw the time I accidentally took the teacher's red pencil home and never returned it, not because I wanted to steal it, but because I was too shy to admit that I had taken it home. I saw the time I sat on an anthill and ran into the house crying because of the ants all over me. I saw my mother brush them off and me going back outside to sit on the anthill again. I saw some scenes of me as a teenager and as a young man. Then Maldorf closed the book and put it back.

"There is one book the Father says I can show you, the book of Abraham's life," he said.

I saw many of the things I knew from Genesis about Abraham, but I also saw things not mentioned in Scripture, like how he and Sarah were very generous and kind with visitors, providing them food, places to sleep, and food and water for their livestock. But then I didn't see any mention of when Abraham lied to Pharaoh telling him that Sarah was his sister, not his wife.

I asked Maldorf, "Where is the other book on Abraham?"

"There is no other."

"But there are some things I know about Abraham from Scripture that I don't see here."

Maldorf explained, "God does not record failures in these records. And furthermore, all record of your sins is wiped from this record the moment you repent, accept Jesus, and are forgiven all those sins."

"Really?" I said, "Does that mean God truly forgets them?"

"Yes. A lady went to her pastor and told him she had a dream and in the dream God told her to tell her pastor He forgives him. The pastor asked for what he was forgiven and she said He didn't say, but she said she will ask if she has another dream. A week later she went back to the pastor and said, 'I had another dream and asked God your question.' 'What did He say?' he asked expectantly. She said God said, 'I don't remember!'"

I commented, "Even though that is a joke, it does show the extent to which God completely forgets what He has forgiven. That is very comforting but far different from the way people usually respond."

At that point I saw an angel take down a book and proceed through it page after page wiping each page with a red cloth. "What is he doing?" I asked.

"That person has just accepted Jesus' forgiveness and the angel is wiping all the entries of sin out of the book. Those pages are now perfectly clean with no trace of the sins left. God cannot find any record of those sins any more. The red cloth represents the blood of Jesus."

I was left speechless at this powerful demonstration of God's love and mercy.

Next we saw the Hall of Knowledge. Maldorf said, "This building is like a library except that whatever knowledge you seek is communicated directly to your mind and spirit."

"Do you mean if I just have a question in my mind, the answer is given to me without looking it up in a book or online?"

"That is right," he said. "And there is no 'online' here. There is no Internet and no need for one. If you need some knowledge it is just given to you. If you need or desire to communicate with someone, you just do it in your mind. All communication is mind to mind, and if you need to be near someone you are suddenly there or quickly travel to the place you need to be. There is no gravity here to hinder your travels and the laws of physics are very different from Earth."

"Are there any books here?" I asked.

"There are some books because some people like to be able to read what they are learning. But most of the knowledge is most easily and quickly transferred in the spirit. Also every book each of God's servants has written is here."

"Is this book I am writing here?"

"Yes, your book is already here and is complete."

"Can I see what I will have written and how it turns out?"

"No, you are not allowed to see anything pertaining to future events. Only God can know those. Even we angels are not allowed to know God's future plans."

"Shucks, it would be nice to know already what I will be writing and not have to think up all of it."

Jacob and Maldorf both chuckled and Jacob said, "Yes, but you will benefit more from having to go through the thinking and creating process. God is more concerned about your growth than the end product."

I saw an absolutely huge and beautiful building in the distance. It seemed to be miles wide and miles high with radiant colored light, thunder, and lightning. "What is that building?" I asked Maldorf.

"That building is where the throne of God is. It is the biggest, most beautiful, most powerful building in heaven. It can be seen from anywhere in heaven."

"Can I see it?"

Jacob said, "yes," so in an instant we were there at the foot of the throne of God in an oval court, several miles wide and long.

I observed, "I can see the gigantic throne shrouded in mist. It has sparkling lights and large columns. There is a cloud of glory over it with thunder, lightning, and an encircling rainbow with more colors than rainbows on Earth. Golden steps are leading up to the throne and there are thousands and millions of souls there praising God and Jesus. There are angels with trumpets that have purple and gold banners on them. The sight itself is beyond comparison with anything on Earth. I can't fully describe what I see. I am aware of a being on the throne who is looking at me with more love in his gaze than I have ever known."

Maldorf explained, "The throne is actually three parts, with God occupying the center part, Jesus the part on the right of God, and Gabriel on the part to the left of God. There are twenty-four other thrones around the throne. Those for the twenty-four elders who are singing praises along with myriads of angels. The four beasts John mentioned are there saying, 'holy, holy, holy.' The people here are so awed by God's power, love, and goodness they can't stop praising Him."

"I wish I could stay here and enjoy this praise and music and joy forever."

But Jacob said, "It is time to go." And then we were instantaneously back where we had been before.

There were many large buildings ahead. I wanted to find out more about them. Maldorf said, "There is a hall of learning in which you can learn anything about what God has done since Creation. There is a building with the written library of God's knowledge. When you pray for wisdom, the Holy Spirit and the angels come here to get God's knowledge that your prayers request. Millions of angels and people come and go at this library.

"There is a Word University where citizens of heaven are taught God's revealed word. Everyone needs to know God's revealed word, and so it is taught to everyone here far beyond anything taught on Earth. Some of the classes are outside, some are inside, some have beanbag chairs, but all are very comfortable and conform to the student's body. Everyone remembers what he/she learns there. There are other universities also.

"There is a place called the Creation Lab. This is a domed building in which are displayed in hologram form scenes from how God accomplished all of creation. This building has the unique feature that there are no entrances. You create an entrance by your faith, but I can't explain how that works. You would have to go there and see it for yourself."

"Can I go and see?"

Jacob said, "No, we have many other things to show you. You can check it out when you come back permanently."

Maldorf said, "There are many other buildings, all very different from what you have on Earth. But one more I want to show you is the building that is being prepared for the Marriage Supper of the Lamb."

We walked past the Hall of Knowledge and turned right. After passing two other buildings we came to a huge building, perhaps as large as three football fields or more. I really couldn't see the other end very well. It is a tall gorgeous building with many stained glass windows. Inside is even more glorious than the outside. It is massive and the architecture is mind-blowing! Even the words "elegant" and "beautiful" don't do it justice. The ceiling is high above the shiny marble floor and tall stained glass windows line the walls. The long tables have pristine white tablecloths with the finest gold china and crystal stemware. Each chair has a name engraved on the inside of the back that was engraved when that person's name was inscribed in the Lamb's Book of Life, according to Maldorf. There are beautiful floral centerpieces and gorgeous golden candelabras. Someone was lighting the candles, which is the last thing you do before the guests arrive.

"Why are they lighting the candles now? Won't they melt before the feast begins?" I asked.

"First of all, the candles will not be consumed because things are not like that here. The candles are being lit with the light of the glory of God, not fire. There is no fire in heaven. Secondly, this feast will begin soon. None of us here know when, only the Father knows. But we can tell it is getting very close to Jesus' return to Earth in power and glory marking the end of the age. All His children will soon be gathered here for this feast in the Lamb's honor. In fact, you are here because God wants you to tell others so no one destined for this banquet will miss it."

"What is that long line of people outside?"

"Those people know the doors are going to open soon and they will be invited in. They are so anxious they can't wait."

My mouth was open in awe. God is not sparing any expense to lavish His love on all His children who have believed His Son and been redeemed by His blood.

As we walked back out of the city, Maldorf explained work in heaven. "Everyone has work to do in heaven. Some, like your Granddad, work out of their homes; others work elsewhere. Everyone is doing something in line with his or her gifts. Each is doing something he or she enjoys, and it serves and glorifies God."

"What do citizens of heaven do for fun or exercise?" I asked.

Maldorf replied, "In heaven you don't need to exercise to stay fit. You can always do whatever you want without getting tired. The only games not available here are ones that belittle someone or cause injury. Competition where one wins and one loses has been replaced with each person or team trying to achieve the best score for Jesus, independently of what the other players or team are able to do. No one loses. If we had more time I could take you to see people riding horses, playing tennis or golf, having a basketball game, throwing horseshoes, or any of a myriad other fun things to do. In each sport we try to honor God, lift up the other person or persons, and do the best we can as a praise to the Father.

"By the Sea of God's Glory there is a place for people who like surfing. Water comes down a mountain to the edge of a lagoon creating 75-foot waves.

"Remember in the park we saw entire families together going places, doing things together, and having happy times with glowing faces. They were having fun. For now I will take you to an amusement park here."

We walked to the other side of the park to the amusement park. I saw a roller coaster that went faster than any on Earth, but it had no wheels! It stayed on the track somehow by the power of God. In another place one can learn to fly without wings. I saw a place where I could sit in my own theater in the Remember When Gallery and review funny, fun-filled, hilarious things that happened in my life. I sat there for a few minutes and laughed a lot. I saw some of the silly things I did as a kid. I saw the time I sneezed eating spaghetti that caused a spaghetti noodle to go up and out my nose. I saw the time I used a Bunsen burner on our gas stove with a test tube from my chemistry set to heat sulfur and paraffin together, causing H_2S to fill the house to the consternation of my parents when they came home. (H_2S is known as the gas that makes a strong rotten egg smell.)

I saw the time my parents gave me a Brownie FunSaver 8mm movie camera for Christmas. The first thing I did with it was to go outside, hold it upside down, and film my brother Charlie doing different things. He walked backwards with empty wrapping paper tubes and dropped them one by one as he walked. Then he held a tennis ball in his hand, opened his hand and let the tennis ball roll out, bounce on the sidewalk and roll into the grass. He bent down to it and snapped his fingers. Then he threw three tennis balls into a bucket. He did other things too. When the film came back I took the leader off, wound it onto another reel, and fastened the leader on the other end. Then we watched the movie. We saw a bucket shake and spit out a tennis ball three times. We saw my brother snap his fingers at a tennis ball and then it started rolling, bounced on the sidewalk, and jumped into his hand. Then as he walked through the yard, empty wrapping paper tubes would jump up into his hand without him looking. It was hilarious. There were many other funny things my brothers and I did together.

Maldorf said, "This is just a glimpse. You are going to have the most amazing time when you live here. You will definitely not be bored but filled with joy and the glory of God in everything you do. His love permeates everything, and I mean everything!"

Jacob said, "It is time for you to go. You have one more appointment and then I will be taking you back."

He took me back along a golden pathway to a building I hadn't seen before. We went in and sat in chairs looking out through a large window directly into Earth.

Jesus appeared before us. He smiled at me with the warmest smile I have ever received and his eyes pierced me with love and complete acceptance. I knew in an instant in that gaze that I was loved more than I could possibly know and all the wrong I had done or good I had not done were completely forgiven and forgotten. I had his total loving acceptance in a way that made me whole and complete like I had never previously experienced. I was totally the way he created me to be without any reservation. I cannot describe the joy that flooded my soul to be in his presence like this.

We talked about many things. I brought up times I knew I had done wrong and he said, "I know, Jacques, there were many times you disappointed me and times you didn't do what I wanted you to. But all those were forgiven when you accepted me into your heart, even the ones that came after that. That never changed my love for you and my desire to bless you and allow you to serve me. I was always with you no matter what you did. I always replaced my disappointment with bringing new ways for you to have joy and to serve me. When you didn't allow me to bless you and use you the way I wanted, I just found other ways to bless and use you after that."

He told me funny things he caused to happen in my life, like the time the spaghetti noodle went out my nose when I sneezed. He said he made that happen because he wanted me to enjoy the life he gave me. Seeing Jesus' joy with me made our time together not only an inspiration but also a very joyful humorous time together. His sense of humor exceeds that of anyone on Earth.

Then we talked about the times I did do what he wanted and he told me more people than I knew were blessed because I gave them a glimpse of him in what I did and shared. He reminded me that along with the vision of how my first wife was full of joy, beauty, healing, and confidence, he had told her to tell me that he was pleased with me. I remembered that and how it blessed me, but now to hear it again from Jesus himself I am humbled to know that God not only loves me, forgives me, and gives me joy, but he is also proud of me. The Lord of all is proud of me! That is more than I have ever expected from God; it is an honor I have trouble believing I deserve. That along with his love and acceptance and joy in my presence continues to be a treasure to my soul.

Even now since I have returned to Earth and am writing this book, the memory of His love and acceptance affects everything I do and is my chief motivation. I really want to please Him since He loves and trusts me so much. I now have an eternal view and my priorities are now based on the remembrance of this time in Jesus' presence. I now know for real that He will take care of me, more than

He takes care of sparrows, no matter what the world or Satan throws at me. I know no one can kill me; they can only free my spirit from my body enabling me to come here forever.

"Jacques, do you see the world out there?" he asked.

"Yes"

"I want you to go back there and tell everyone you can about this visit. I am coming back very soon to take all my own to be with me and to sit down at the celebration supper of the Lamb. I want them to know how wonderful my preparations for them are so no one that I love and died to save will miss this. My Father does not allow any anger, hate, greed, jealousy, envy, covetousness, or anything unloving here to spoil the beauty of this place. I will be with you as you write this story and I will be with you and open doors for you to tell it. I love you my dear Jacques. You are a good servant and you bless me."

"I don't know what to say. I am floored at how much you love me and accept me, even flawed old me. I will tell this story and look for the doors you will open to tell this story. I can't thank you enough for all you have given me."

With that He hugged me. Jacob took my hand and we beamed out the window toward the Earth I saw.

A WALK THROUGH HEAVEN

"I never thanked Maldorf!" I exclaimed.

"That is okay. He knows," Jacob replied.

We arrived back beside my bed with the lump still in it.

"Thanks, Jacob, for all you have done for me."

"I am your guardian angel. I have been with you since you were conceived and I will be with you until I take you to heaven for you to occupy your eternal home. I will be watching out for you every hour and every day, even if you are not aware of my presence. But if you have any need, speak to the Father, not to me. He will direct me how to help or answer you. God bless you Jacques."

And he was gone from my sight.

I lay down on my physical body, back to chest, arm to arm, leg to leg, and head to head. My spirit slid smoothly back into my physical body and I was asleep.

Later I woke up and thought, "What a strange and wonderful dream I just had. Did I really see heaven or just dream it. If it was a dream, it was very thorough and realistic." But I could find no evidence that I had been gone. I checked my eyes and my hand and my healings are yet to come. So maybe I will never know if it was real or not. On the other hand, I can tell something is different. I feel more peace and I have a sense of cleanness and wholeness I have not known before and can't really describe. Maybe I really have bathed in the River of Life and the Sea of God's Glory and been in Jesus' presence. In any case, I better write this story like Jesus said.

P.S. For a more complete account of what heaven is like read *Heaven Is Beyond Imagination*.

[For copies, comment, or info contact Dr.JELaFrance@gmail.com]

Index of Topics

How It All Began — 1
Jacob, My Guardian Angel — 3
First Views — 5
A Great Cloud of Witnesses — 8
Plants in Heaven — 12
Pets and Animals — 17
Children — 20
The River of Life — 24
Music — 27
Landscapes — 30
The City and Streets — 32
Mansions — 33
Great Buildings — 36
The Throne of God — 38
The Marriage Supper Building — 40
Work and Recreation — 41
Meeting Jesus — 42
Back Home — 46

www.ingramcontent.com/pod-product-compliance
Lightning Source LLC
LaVergne TN
LVHW010620070526
838199LV00063BA/5212